BRIDGE

THE ALTERNATIVE

BRIDGE

PATRICK JONES

MINNEAPOLIS

Darby Creek
A division of Lerner Publishing Group, Inc.
241 First Avenue North
Minneapolis, MN 55401 USA

For updated reading levels and more information, look up this title at www.lernerbooks.com.

Cover and interior photographs © Dale May/CORBIS (boy);
© iStockphoto.com/joeygil (locker background).

Main body text set in Janson Text LT Std 12/17.5.
Typeface provided by Linotype AG.

Library of Congress Cataloging-in-Publication Data

Jones, Patrick, 1961–
    Bridge / by Patrick Jones.
        pages   cm. — (The alternative)
    Summary: Eighteen-year-old José serves as the bridge between his non-English-speaking family and the rest of the world, and because his parents are illegal immigrants and extended family lives with them, money is tight, so José works nights and arrives at school so tired that teachers at his alternative high school step in to help.
    ISBN 978–1–4677–3903–0 (lib. bdg. : alk. paper)
    ISBN 978–1–4677–4636–6 (eBook)
    [1. Work—Fiction. 2. Spanish language—Fiction. 3. High schools—Fiction. 4. Schools—Fiction. 5. Illegal aliens—Fiction. 6. Hispanic Americans—Fiction.] I. Title.
PZ7.J7242Bri 2014
[Fic]—dc23   2013041390

Manufactured in the United States of America
1 – BP – 7/15/14

WITH THANKS TO ANALEYSHA,
KIARA, AND NAYALIE
-P.J.

1

EARLY MORNING / MONDAY, JANUARY 6
ST. PAUL, MINNESOTA

It was six in the morning when José discovered his *pinche* Chevy Impala wouldn't start.

José turned the key, but there was no roar. Just the sputter of the ten-year-old car's failing engine on a frozen Minnesota morning. In the familiar driver's seat, José cursed in Spanish and thought about everything he needed his car for that day. School, working second shift stocking groceries at Rainbow Foods, and handling whatever crisis of the day came up at home. He was jammed in a two-bedroom apartment with his always-exhausted mom, his disabled dad, his frantic aunt and her two young children, seven statues of the Virgin Mary, and one hundred plastic flowers, so it was always something.

If the Chevy wouldn't start, it meant a long bus ride to school for José. It also meant bus rides for his mom, to the first of her two jobs, and his dad, to physical therapy. José checked his phone. He thought about calling his best friend Tony for a ride and decided no, only in an emergency. *Except my life has seemed like one long emergency for the past ten years*, José thought.

José set his phone on the torn and frayed passenger seat, grabbed the ice scraper, and headed into the cold with his thin coat and a red wool cap to keep him warm. As he scraped the windshield, he wondered why his parents had left the warmth of Mexico for the cold of Minnesota. At school he'd always wanted to ask the Somali, Hmong, and other Latino students the same question: What were our parents thinking, moving to this icebox?

The scraping sound on the stubborn frost seemed louder than normal in the quiet of the early morning. José scraped the other windows with alternating hands, switching as each arm got tired. He knew too well from his dad how much losing the ability to use one hand mattered.

Even in the cold, José worked up a sweat removing the ice from the windows. Back inside the car, he tried the engine one last time, hoping somehow that clearing the ice would make a difference, but nothing. Maybe his mom could pray the car would start, he thought, as she prayed for everything.

José picked up his phone and found the numbers he'd need to call between classes: the Metro Mobility van, to pick up his dad; the landlord, about the rent being late again; and the pharmacy, to tell them they had messed up the medicine for his aunt's oldest kid. José would need to communicate for her, as he had to for most appointments and other errands, because he was the only fluent English speaker in his house. His unlimited phone minutes were filled with unlimited tasks, translating and beyond, for his family.

As he thought about going back to school one last time, José wondered if he could stand the stress. At what point, he asked himself, would he buckle under the pressure?

2

"Do we understand each other, José?" Mrs. Baker asked. She sat at her desk, looking very much in charge of the school. José stood in front of her, head bowed, his red cap in his hand. "This is your fourth try here at Rondo, but I'm afraid it's your last chance."

José nodded. He came to the school in ninth grade, already behind in credits. That was five years ago. Most of the people he'd started with had come, graduated, and gone. Twice, he'd dropped out when his Aunt Cecilia had her babies and needed the help around the house. This past fall José had left Rondo after six weeks to work a full-time third-shift job at UPS in addition to his part-time job at Rainbow. He'd grown stronger muscles, but also stronger determination to graduate and go to college.

"I know you're over eighteen," Mrs. Baker continued, "but I hope you've had your parents read the contract." José said nothing. They hadn't read it because it was in English. Besides, "contract" sounded like a legal document, something his undocumented parents would want nothing to do with. "The contract commits you to finish the school year. You've given me your word." José nodded and held out the paper.

Mrs. Baker took the contract from José's hand and signed her name at the bottom. Then she motioned for José to sit in the chair in front of her desk. She sounded impatient—not as caring and concerned as he remembered the teachers and staff at Rondo.

"What about your Personal Education Plan?" she asked. José unfolded the sheet of paper from the back pocket of his jeans. He handed it to Mrs. Baker, who slowly smoothed it out as she scanned it.

"These are fine goals," Mrs. Baker said. "Earn all your credits, earn at least one A, and attend the after-school tutoring program whenever possible."

"I can do it this time," José said, embarrassed by his past failures.

"Good, but let's modify your behavior goals."

José frowned.

"You say 'Come to school every day.' That's a high standard, compared to your past performance. What I've seen from you is that if you do miss a day, then you get down on yourself, which causes you to miss more school, and before you know it, you've dropped out again. Let's change that."

"What would you suggest?" José asked.

Mrs. Baker hesitated. "What would *you* suggest, José?"

José turned silent. After thinking for a minute, he said, "How about, come to school at least four days a week and be on time those days?" Mrs. Baker wrote the new language on the paper.

"And I like this goal of not falling asleep in class as much," Mrs. Baker said. "But how do you plan to do that? I know you earn credits for holding a job, so what will be different?"

Another silence. Then, "I'll get more sleep." Like that was possible. His small sofa bed didn't lend itself to restful nights. But it was the only thing José could think of to say.

Mrs. Baker looked skeptical. "Keep thinking on that. But the last one is excellent." José smiled at the compliment, even if the last goal would be the hardest: talk more in class. He felt he already did plenty of talking as the voice of four people at home.

"Is Mrs. Howard-Hernandez going to be my coach?" José asked. Every student had a coach to help keep them on track.

"No, I've got someone else in mind."

"Who?"

"Me," Mrs. Baker said. "I am personally committed to helping you graduate."

"*Gracias*," José said. "So, what do you think of my future goals?"

Mrs. Baker examined the paper. "Good, except you only listed one, not three. Why?"

"Going to college is my top priority," José said. "Nothing else matters but that." His parents' hard lives, with little education, had committed José to his dream of graduating from college. The clock was ticking—you couldn't attend Rondo after age twenty-one—and José knew he needed to focus on school, earn his credits, get his diploma, and get into college somewhere. With the Dream Act in Minnesota, it wouldn't matter that his parents had fake green cards after overstaying their visas many years ago. José would be able to get financial aid for college. He'd be one step closer to getting his degree and a better life.

3

Late morning / Monday, January 6
Mrs. Howard-Hernandez's classroom

"Hey, cuz," Tony said when José walked into language arts. Tony had been José's best friend for years and was more like a cousin to José than some of his extended family.

Fist bumps and back slaps finished the greeting. "Hey, Mia," José said.

"Hey yourself, sleepyhead," she replied as José couldn't hide a yawn. Mia was Tony's cousin and one of the prettiest girls at Rondo, but José kept his distance. A girl like Mia deserved a man's full attention, which José couldn't offer with all his other responsibilities.

"Good morning, everyone," Mrs. Howard-Hernandez said. "It's nice to see all of you back from winter break. And a special welcome back to José Gomez."

A few people applauded, and José shot them an embarrassed wave.

"We've got a lot of work with this new unit, so hang on to your hats!" The teacher's corny line drew some laughter, maybe because Rondo actually let students wear hats in class. "Today, we'll start the book *The Things They Carried*, by author Tim O'Brien. This is probably the best book written by an American about the Vietnam War."

People jumped in with questions about the book, the assignments, and how they'd be graded. Then Tony asked, "What's the Vietnam War?" Groans followed.

While Mrs. Howard-Hernandez explained the basics of the war, she had Jake and Monica pass out copies of the book. Once everyone had one, she asked the students to follow along as she read. José struggled to keep his eyes open and not fail one of his goals on the first day.

"OK everyone, before we read any further, put your books down and open your notebooks. What are the things you carry with you? Open your purses, bags, and wallets, and write down the list."

As papers rustled, Jake shouted, "How do you spell *condom*?" Mia blushed, Tony frowned, and the teacher shook her head. Similar spelling questions about weed, types of guns, and vodka followed. José knew some were just showing off, but for other people, those were *exactly* the things they carried.

In his bag, José had the normal trappings of any student, and one extra book: his old Spanish and English dictionary. *If only I'd had one when Dad got hurt*, José thought, *everything would be different now.* When the teacher asked people to share their lists, José didn't raise his hand.

Mrs. Howard-Hernandez broke the class into small groups and then read the next section, about a soldier who carried a hatchet as a symbol of his culture. "What objects do you carry because you're part of something else, like your culture, your family, or your friends at school?" she asked.

José had to push himself to talk, even with Tony, Mia, and Jake in his group. They knew about his family and his dad's accident, or at least most of the story. After the teacher read another passage, she put the book down and addressed the class again. "Now, here's a slightly different question: what are the emotional things you carry?"

For José, the response to this question wasn't one he'd share even with his best friends. It was a simple three-word answer: shame, guilt, and regret. Yet it weighed José down, carrying those three words and the secret he'd kept for ten years.

4

"José, you're needed in the principal's office!" José's fourth-grade teacher announced, causing a ripple of laughter through the classroom. He'd been to the office before, and it was never good. As he picked up his books and headed out into the hall, José couldn't figure out what he'd done wrong. His last fight was a month ago, with a kid who insulted his heritage. And he was doing well at school, working hard—he thought he was a model student.

When he walked through the door, he was sur-prised to see his mother standing there, tears in her eyes. "Mamá, ¿qué pasó?" *José asked. The office lady seemed to be listening in, although she spoke only English; he'd seen her do it before whenever he spoke with the other Hispanic students in Spanish.*

"Tu papá tuvo un accidente."

An accident? José started to ask another ques-tion, but his mom grabbed him by the hand and almost pulled him out the door. He barely heard the women in office yelling at them ("You need to sign him out!") because of his mom's heavy sobs and fran-tic shouts of "Rápido, rápido."

José felt nervous with his mother driving their new Chevy, since normally his dad drove the family everywhere, including trips from their town of Ben-son to Minneapolis to see his uncle. That two-hour-plus drive seemed short compared to the eternity it took to drive the few miles from school to Dad's worksite. José stayed quiet so he wouldn't distract his mom.

At the worksite, José saw the white van and trucks of the roofing company, but no people. His mom parked, and together they raced toward the house. As José got closer, he heard a familiar voice: his dad's foreman speaking in broken Spanish, telling everyone to get back to work. When he rounded the corner, José saw all the men standing in a large group. As the foreman yelled more, the workers walked slowly back toward their ladders. Except for José's father, who lay with the left side of his face resting against the concrete porch slab, breathing heavily.

5

Using his cane, José's father pointed at the small piece of metal under a snow-covered tree. During the week, his father would take a bus to various places around St. Paul and look for scrap metal. He'd write down in a small notebook where he found pieces. Another man might be able to remember, but his short-term memory wasn't so good. José's father could recall vivid details of his childhood in Taxco, an old mining town between Mexico City and Acapulco. He could remember José's childhood in Benson, but not what he ate for dinner the day before.

José located the metal, put on gloves, placed the metal in the bag, and returned to his dad's side. Slowly, the two men moved through the snow. His dad's right leg dragged behind. "How is school?" his dad asked in Spanish. José's dad had made it only through fourth grade.

"It's hard because there's so much work and so little time," José explained. It was easy for José to talk with his dad. It was almost like keeping a diary that nobody else read. His father wouldn't remember most of what José told him, so he could tell his dad almost anything.

Every now and then, his father would nod as if he understood. José was telling him with some excitement about the book they were reading when his father stopped. He pulled the notebook out of his front pocket, balanced it against his chest, and opened the pages. When he tried to turn the page, the black notebook dropped into the white snow. His father cursed, his only bad habit. Every now and then, he'd do it in front of one of the Virgin Mary statues and cause a big fight with José's mom.

José picked up the notebook, quickly dried off the pages on the edge of his sweatshirt, and found the page his father wanted. There was an address and a badly drawn picture. He laughed to himself. Other dads took their kids skiing or sledding, but José's was probably the only one who took his son scrapping.

They didn't say much until they reached the address, a burned-out house. Following his father's instructions, José climbed over the fence, located the twisted piece of metal, and returned with a big smile on his face, only to find his father crying, as he often did for no reason.

"*Papá, ¿estás bien?*" José asked and then handed his father the scrap metal.

His father just wiped his tears and nodded, thanked José, and turned back to his notebook.

Two hours later, when José and his dad walked in with their twenty-dollar scrap metal score, his mom and Aunt Cecilia were screaming at each other in Spanish. It was the same fight they'd had most every day since Cecilia showed up at their doorstep six years ago, in part to help with José's father. Almost immediately some *vaquero* with snakeskin boots and snake-charmer words got her pregnant. It repeated a few years later. Many times in between and since, she'd had this argument with José's mom: would Cecilia make the same mistake again, or would she get it right?

In the background, José heard his cousins crying. The crying grew louder when his aunt slammed the apartment door. José's mother folded her hands in prayer, mumbled some words to a statue of the Virgin, and went into Cecilia's room to comfort the children. When she came out with a child clinging to each shoulder, José asked her why she put up with such bad behavior.

Over the crying children, José's mother said softly, *"Porque somos familia, hijo."*

José hated Mondays, listening to everybody tell their stories about parties, dances, movies, and all the things he didn't have time for. He worked second shift stocking groceries both Saturdays and Sundays. It was hard labor for little money. But every canned good he lifted, José understood, was one step closer to affording college.

"Stay awake today, cuz," Tony joked just before class started. He'd blown it last Friday, but luckily Tony had caught him napping before the teacher did. "Your snoring distracts me too much."

José toasted Tony with his energy drink. "Your ugly face distracts me."

The two friends traded friendly insults—clean ones in English, dirty ones in Spanish—until Mrs. Howard-Hernandez called them out, in Spanish, to remind them she knew exactly what they were saying.

"Take out *The Things They Carried*. We'll start today with the story "On the Rainy River." Would anyone like to read?"

"I'll do it," Jake said, earning a proud smile from his teacher. Jake read a few pages of the story until someone else volunteered. José found the book hard to follow because it wasn't really a novel, but a series of stories. And it was supposed to be fiction, but the main character's name was Tim O'Brien, the author's name.

Mrs. Howard-Hernandez read the last line of the story over again—"I was a coward; I went to war"—and repeated it another time. Then she said, "Let's break up into pairs and discuss that."

Jake latched onto Mia, so Tony and José paired up as always.

"Tim had to decide," Mrs. Howard-Hernandez continued, "either go to Vietnam and fight for his country, or flee to Canada and avoid the draft to stay alive. He decided to fight. Right or wrong? Talk about it in pairs, and then we'll debate it as a large group in a few minutes."

"They don't do that anymore do they? A draft, where they make you go to war, right?" Tony asked the teacher. Like José, Tony was over eighteen and, if there was a draft, probably eligible.

"No, it is a volunteer military, so no, there's no draft."

Tony leaned toward José. "I wouldn't go. I don't like people telling me what to do."

José laughed. "You can't run away from your responsibilities."

Tony wasn't laughing. "Why not? My father did; so did Jake's pop. Half the kids here got no dad at home."

For a second, José envied Tony. Every time José quit school, he thought about running away from his family and all of the responsibility he'd inherited so young.

"If somebody attacked me or my family or my country, I'd fight," Tony said. "But from what we learned about the war, that didn't happen. I wouldn't kill people who didn't hurt me."

As José thought about his answer, he felt a splitting headache start. But he gulped down an energy drink and fought through the pain.

"Cuz, how many of those you doing a day?" Tony asked.

José shrugged. "I lost count." Tony slapped José on the back and laughed.

"So, Tony and José, what have you decided?" asked Mr. Aaron, the educational assistant with great gray dreads. Tony explained his position, which boiled down to staying alive at all costs.

"I don't know," José said when Mr. Aaron turned to him. "If you're born in the US, you should fight for it, you shouldn't have a choice. Like your family, you didn't get a choice. You just do whatever you have to do to protect it."

7

José's dad climbed slowly into the car, starting to tell another story from his childhood. José seethed in anger that once again, his dad had missed the Metro Mobility bus home. José was never really off duty on his day off.

"How was rehab?" José asked sharply. His father said nothing. He didn't remember.

"You seem to have some strength coming in your right arm," José said, mostly a lie. If there was any difference, it was like changing from a D– to a D.

"I want to work again." The expression on his dad's face was a half-frown, as always. The droopiness on the right side was permanent.

"You were going to tell me about growing up," José said, changing the subject. He knew telling stories about growing up in Taxco brought joy to his dad.

When they got back home, they opened the door to the sound of adults shouting and children crying.

"*¿Quién te va a cuidar a los niños?*" José's mom asked. From the way Cecilia was dressed—high heels, low-cut dress—it was clear she wasn't staying home to watch her children.

"José," Cecilia answered, not as question, but as a fact. She picked up her black purse.

"*¡A ver si puedes cerrar las piernas esta vez!*" José's mom shouted. Whenever Cecilia left the house, José's mother always said something like that: Keep your legs closed this time.

Back and forth the sisters yelled at each other, while Cecilia's children bawled from the other room. A neighbor pounded on the wall. José stood frozen for minutes, until finally he shouted, louder than any other sound. *"Mamá, Cecilia, ¡basta, ya párenle!"* Stop it!

But it didn't matter which language he spoke, his mother and aunt were in no mood to listen. The neighbor pounded on the wall again for quiet.

"José, ven aquí por favor." José heard his father call from his bedroom.

His father sat at the foot of the bed. At his feet, Cecilia's children cuddled silently. On his lap José's father balanced an oversized book. An old photo album.

"Look at them." José's dad pointed at a photo of his mom's family. In the photo, José's mom cradled her baby sister in her arms. In the other room, the shouting continued.

"Why can't things be like they were, not like they are?" José's dad muttered in Spanish, quieter but more powerful than any scream. José left his dad, grabbed his books, and fled.

José got lucky and found an empty study carrel at the Metro State University Library. He liked sitting in a college library; he was living his future a few minutes at a time. José leaned back in his chair and pulled out *The Things They Carried*. He liked how it usually distracted him from his real life. But that night, his father's question kept ringing in his ears: *Why can't things be like they were?* Deep down, José knew the answer.

8

TEN YEARS EARLIER, LATE SPRING
BENSON, MINNESOTA

"Get him out of here!" the foreman shouted at José, at the same time that José's mother was shouting questions for José to ask the foreman.

"What happened?" José asked the foreman, who towered over the ten-year-old boy.

"What do you think?" the foreman replied. He nodded toward José's mother. "Tell her to quiet down. She's giving me a headache."

José's mom wouldn't stop firing questions at

José, who had to recall what his mom said, ask the foreman, get the answer, and translate back to his mom. Meanwhile, José tried not to get distracted by his dad, who kept trying to stand up but failing. "She wants to know why he's on the ground."

"It's his own fault. He showed up drunk and tripped," the foreman said. José relayed the information to his mom, who helped his father up. His father's eyes had an odd, far-off look.

His mom was firing off more for José to translate. It was hard to keep up with the adult questions he didn't understand. "She says he doesn't drink. She says it's your job to keep him safe. How is tripping his fault?"

The foreman just looked away and shook his head, which struck José as odd.

"¡Ambulancia!" José's mom yelled.

"And who has the pesos for an ambulancia?" the foreman said. His tone made José nervous.

When José's dad regained his feet, he tried to talk, but he slurred his words. Yet it was clear he didn't want an ambulance. He took another step away from the house, then bent over and vomited in the grass.

"You see? Look, I don't know if he's still drunk or just hungover like most of these guys. But he can't stay on my worksite."

"Drunk?" José had seen people drunk, and they did behave kind of like this, but he knew his father didn't drink. He complained all the time about coworkers who did. But if he wasn't drunk, José wondered as his dad finally made it to the Chevy, then what was wrong with him?

9

LATE MORNING / TUESDAY, JANUARY 21
MRS. HOWARD-HERNANDEZ'S CLASSROOM

"He had it easy," José mumbled under his breath to Tony. Mrs. Howard-Hernandez was reading the story "The Dentist," which described the typical stress-filled day of a soldier in Vietnam.

"Right, except for the life and death part," Tony cracked back.

"Maybe," José mumbled. He gulped another energy drink and tried to stay focused.

As other students answered the teacher's

questions about a typical day, José thought about how his typical day wasn't long enough, or at least didn't allow enough time for sleep. He'd worked eight hours every day over the weekend at Rainbow, and then he worked two nights at UPS as an emergency fill-in. When he'd quit UPS after Christmas, his boss, Mr. Harmon—a pretty nice guy, José thought—told him it was too much paperwork, so he'd just keep him on the payroll as a temporary worker and "if you want work every now and then, you let me know." So he did.

Mrs. Howard-Hernandez started to read from the book again. "This part is called 'How to Tell a War Story,'" she started. "After we've read it, you'll break into groups . . ."

José pulled his hat over his eyes. They'd stay open, then they'd shut. His head would pitch forward, then he'd pull it back. Like he'd learned about Vietnam, fighting his tiredness was a war of attrition that, in the end, he couldn't win.

❂ ❂ ❂

When the bell rang to end language arts and

woke José, Mr. Aaron told him to report to Mrs. Baker's office. "Lots of people sleep in class," José told Mrs. Baker. She wasn't moved.

"But those people didn't make it a specific goal not to fall asleep in class."

"I know, I'm sorry."

Mrs. Baker bounced a pencil up and down against the desk. "José, that's not enough."

"What else do you want from me?" José asked quietly, but he wanted to scream the words. Not just at Mrs. Baker, but at this family. *Everybody takes from me*, José thought, *but nobody gives.*

"I want to know what your plan is," Mrs. Baker snapped, like his mom did when angry.

"We already went over it."

Mrs. Baker clicked the mouse on her computer and looked at something on her screen. "Your plan lists what goals you want to achieve, but we need to talk about how you plan to achieve them. You said that you'd get more sleep at home, yet once again. . . And I understand it is not just in one class, but in all of them." José's head dropped, not in exhaustion, but in shame.

"Look, it's really complicated."

Mrs. Baker turned off the screen and leaned across her desk. "José, everybody's life in this school is complicated, that's why they're at Rondo. It's not an excuse."

"I'll try to do better, really. I'll make up the work from today."

"OK, let's do that right now," Mrs. Baker said. "The group assignment today, I've learned, was to discuss telling memories as stories, and how the stories change over time as they're told and retold."

"I guess." He'd fallen asleep before that. He was angry at himself, but also at Jake, Mia, and Tony for letting him sleep. Like fellow soldiers, they were supposed to have his back.

"So, do you have any stories like that in your life, José?" Mrs. Baker asked.

José closed his eyes to concentrate on the one that came to mind. José wished he could change the story and be the hero in the story instead of the villain. "Not really."

"José, think of one and tell it to me tomorrow."

José said nothing—he knew silence was the only weapon he could use right then.

Mrs. Baker turned back to her computer. "José, you're free to go."

10

José huddled in the corner of the furnished basement at his Uncle Mandy's house, playing video games and talking with his cousin Carlos. Carlos was a junior in college. He'd spent his first two years at Metro State but had transferred to the University of Minnesota. That was the path José thought he'd take. Except that, once done with Metro State and his generals, he'd go someplace else. Someplace out of state, maybe Texas or California. Someplace warm and far away.

"You still at Rondo?" Carlos asked. It seemed to José that when he said the word *still* there was an edge to it.

"Yes, but this time, I'm sticking with it." José tried to sound confident, determined.

"That's good," Carlos said. "The world doesn't need more uneducated and unemployed Latinos making all of us look bad."

You're talking about my dad, José thought, *and I know it.*

"You still working too?"

José nodded.

"That's hard, but I know all about that."

José looked at his cousin's hands. Not a scratch on them. He laughed to himself.

"Okay, next round," Carlos said. José was glad to focus on the video game. "Cuz, I'm smoking you!" Carlos shouted.

José said nothing as he played the game, more by instinct than interest. Like life, video games were all about choices. As bodies fell around him, José thought about the story he'd written for Mrs. Baker, about his father and his uncle coming north and how two brothers had lived such different lives.

After his dad and uncle had left the beet fields of northern Minnesota, his father followed some friends to Benson to work in a small factory. But it got raided, and his dad barely made it out free. After that, he found work with the roofing company. He loved it—until the accident. Then they moved to St. Paul, where Uncle Mandy lived. After Mandy had left the fields, he'd moved to the big city, where he got two things: a GED and a legit green card for marrying a US citizen. Since then, he'd prospered and gotten more education, and now he ran a small trucking company while his wife worked for the state in an office job. Both of his sons were in college, with Carlos at the U and the older son, Miguel, in his first year of the MBA program at the University of Pennsylvania.

"Cuz, what's wrong with you?" Carlos asked. He was killing José in the game.

"Sorry, I just got a lot on my mind," José

answered. He told Carlos about balancing school, work, and family duties, hoping for maybe empathy, if not sympathy.

"Tell me about it," Carlos replied and then listed his problems, all of them small.

Upstairs, José heard people laughing and speaking, but mostly in English. Uncle Mandy didn't use much Spanish in his house. José knew that meant his mom and dad felt as left out upstairs as he did in the basement.

"The key is getting that money," Carlos said, stating the obvious. Even the basement of the small house seemed huge to José, compared to his tiny apartment.

"Go again?" Carlos asked.

José nodded. "In a minute, I gotta make a call." José pulled himself from the comfortable sofa, away from the big-screen TV and the new Xbox, and walked toward the downstairs bathroom. If he took more hours at UPS, his family could afford some of those luxuries too. He closed the bathroom door behind him and hit a key. The temptation of those ten digits shouted José's name: his UPS boss's number.

He stared at the screen for a full minute before he put the phone away again.

11

TEN YEARS EARLIER, LATE SPRING
BENSON, MINNESOTA

"Intoxicado," *José's dad kept repeating as he lay in the backseat of the Chevy. They'd taken him home as he'd asked, but finally José's dad relented and allowed his wife to take him to the small hospital in Benson. He kept his right hand on his stomach and his left clutching his head. José guessed it was something more than an upset stomach. Maybe his dad had food poisoning.*

The small emergency room was empty. Two

nurses sat at the desk. José's dad leaned on him for support, but his mom raced ahead. By the time she reached the nurses' desk, she was shouting for help for her husband.

The nurses looked at each other and then toward José. José's dad stumbled as he approached the desk and began talking. But even if the nurses spoke Spanish, they wouldn't have understood his slurred words, repeating the same phrases over and over.

"English?" the older nurse asked.

"I speak English," José said over his dad's increased volume of blabbering.

"What's wrong with him?" the nurse asked.

José told the story about finding his father face-down at the work site. The two nurses didn't seem concerned, but asked José questions that he didn't really know how to answer.

"What is he saying?" the younger nurse asked. José's dad was now shouting one word.

"Intoxicado," José answered, repeating the Spanish more clearly. He hadn't yet learned the words it translated to in English: nauseated, or sick from food. But the nurse raised an eyebrow like he had told her what she needed to know.

The older nurse picked up a phone, dialed quickly, and spoke with her hand over the receiver. "Take a seat," the young nurse said. José explained to his parents what she'd said.

José sat with his parents, waiting for the doctor. José breathed in relief when the door finally opened, except the uniforms were not that of a doctor or nurse, but rather of two police officers.

12

José clutched the pencil like a drowning man hanging onto a life raft in the ocean. He'd told Mrs. Baker he would get an A in at least one class, and he knew language arts was his only hope. After missing school for chunks of time, it was hard to get caught up in his science or math classes. *I'm so far behind*, José thought, *I should drop out again.*

"For this test, there are fifteen short-answer

questions, each worth five points," Mrs. Howard-Hernandez said to the quiet room. "And one essay question worth twenty-five points."

"I don't get it," Tony said. "I mean the essay question, can you explain it?"

José glanced at the test in front of him. It was over the two of the hardest stories in the book: "Speaking of Courage" and "Notes." When his teacher had read them aloud in class, it was quiet like now—except for a few people in the class sniffling and wiping away tears.

"Tim's friend Norman was trying to reach out for help. How did he succeed? How did he not? Should Tim be held responsible for Norman's suicide since Tim was the one he reached out to for help? And finally, relate it to your life. Write about a time when someone needed your help, and say how you reacted."

José raced through the short-answer questions. Not only had he read those stories on his own more than once, but he'd researched them at the library. But when José reached the essay question, he went blank. It was too personal. He suddenly felt sick. *Intoxicado.*

A wave of nausea raced through José. Without a word, he raced for the front of the room, snatched the bathroom pass/key, and ran down the hall toward the bathroom. He barely made it into the stall before the contents of his stomach emptied. Beads of sweat ran down José's face from beneath the red wool cap still on his head. He wiped his mouth, flushed the toilet, and started to stand, but as if he'd been smacked with a hammer—or fallen off a ladder—he couldn't move.

On the dirty floor of the Rondo bathroom, José allowed himself to cry. He cried for himself, his family, his future. After a few minutes, José heard the door open.

"José, are you okay?" It was Mr. Aaron.

José stared at the floor, composing himself. "Yes," he replied after a minute. "Yes." He was okay. His future would be too.

◊ ◊ ◊

"*José, te necesito!*" José heard his mother shout from his parents' bedroom. He sat at the kitchen table, putting the final touches on the essay that his teacher had let him finish at home.

José raced to bedroom to find his father on the floor, unconscious. *"Mamá, ¿qué pasó?"*

José's mother explained that his father had been reaching for something on the top shelf of their closet when he lost his balance and fell awkwardly onto the floor. José could tell his father was breathing, but his eyes were closed. He dialed 911 without asking or thinking. This time there would be no misunderstanding. José explained that his father had hit his head and needed an ambulance. He spoke calmly, confidently.

José stayed by his father's side as they waited for the ambulance. In the other room, he heard his mom praying and his aunt making calls, trying to find someone to watch her children.

José wiped the trickle of blood from his father's nose. When he touched his father's misshapen face, José's father's eyes opened slowly. *"Papi, ¿estás bien?"* José asked.

To José it looked like his dad was trying to smile but couldn't, like he was trying to assure José. When his dad started to speak, José put a finger softly against his lips. His dad said nothing else; instead he reached out his left arm toward José, asking for help.

José let his dad wrap his left arm around his shoulders, strong from throwing boxes, stacking cans, and carrying the weight for his family, and he pulled his father up.

13

Unlike the hospital in Benson, the emergency room at Regions was crowded with faces of all colors, both patients and staff. On the walls, signs were in English, Spanish, Somali, and Hmong, the four languages spoken most in St. Paul.

After the ambulance left with José's parents, José and his aunt drove to Tony's house, where Tony and his mom agreed to watch Cecilia's children. When they arrived at the hospital, his parents were nowhere to be seen. José waited his turn and approached the desk.

"Pepe Gomez? I'm his son. Where is he?" José asked. The nurse explained that his father had been admitted and was waiting for a doctor. "Can I see him?"

The nurse nodded. "First, we need some information, OK?" The nurse pushed a clipboard filled with forms across the desk. "Your mother was too upset to fill them out."

The forms were in English, which José realized might have been the real reason. He took the clipboard and sat next to his aunt.

José had to leave many blanks empty: his dad's employer, insurance, medications, doctor's name, social security number, driver's license. *My dad's life*, José thought, *is a blank form.*

After he handed in the form, he returned to sit next to his aunt. She was crying. José tried to comfort her, but it seemed to only make things worse. She'd start to speak and then have to stop. When Cecilia did speak, she used the volume she was most accustomed to in talking with her children and arguing with her older sister: loud.

Cecilia finally composed herself, wiped her tears, and apologized to José in the tone of a confession.

"*Todo va a estar bien,*" José replied, and said it again in English. "It's going to be okay."

Cecilia didn't argue. She just continued telling José how sorry and ashamed she was for her actions and how she treated José's mother. With deep emotion in her voice, José's aunt talked about feeling trapped—first in Mexico, by poverty, and then in the US, by her own bad choices. "*Todo va a estar bien,*" José repeated.

"José Gomez?" a nurse called out. José almost ran to the desk. "The doctor wants to talk with you. Come this way, please." José followed the nurse, fear building with each step.

The nurse walked too slowly for José along a line of closed blue drapes. Near the end of the hall, she pulled back the drape. José saw his father sitting up in the bed. There was another nurse, a doctor, and young woman speaking to José's mom in Spanish.

"We need some medical history, José," the

nurse said, flipping a few pages in his notes. "Has your father had a stroke?"

"No . . . about ten years ago he fell off a ladder at work and hit his head on the ground."

"His left side, correct?" the doctor asked. José nodded. How did she know that?

"After he fell the first time, did things get back to normal?" the doctor continued.

José answered no, and the doctor nodded like she'd expected that.

"So he was never quite the same, and then he fell again today."

José nodded again to confirm.

"Back when he fell before, he probably suffered a traumatic brain injury," the doctor explained. "I hope he got medical treatment for that. Do you remember, at the hospital, what—"

"He didn't get treated at the hospital right away," José said, his shame overwhelming him.

"Why not?"

José paused. He could lie to the doctor and tell him it was because they didn't have money or because he was undocumented, but he knew he needed to tell the truth.

"He kept repeating *'intoxicado,'* so that's the word I told them. They took him to jail. They thought he was drunk."

14

TEN YEARS EARLIER, LATE SPRING
BENSON, MINNESOTA

*Just like every day since he father was moved from
the county jail to the hospital, José and his mom stood
next to the bed. His mom clutched her rosary; José
held his father's limp right hand. The beeping sounds
of modern medical machines drowned out his mom's
mumbled prayers. The lines of the screens moved, but
his dad didn't. He was in a coma for the third day.*

*Exhausted, José sat in the small, hard chair next
to the bed. Other than going to the bathroom, he*

hadn't left his father's side—or, just as importantly, his mom's. She needed him, not just for support, but in case the doctor came in to explain what was going on. But other than nurses coming and going, no other medical personnel had entered the room. The Hispanic janitors helped by answering questions and bringing snacks for José to eat. His mom had refused food, telling José she would eat again when her husband could eat, not one second before.

His dad's friends from work brought José meals and stayed for short periods of time. They told José how the foreman hadn't reported that his dad had fallen from a ladder. The foreman had told everyone on the crew that José's dad was drunk and that's why he fell. Oscar, his dad's best friend at work, confirmed what José knew in his heart: his dad hadn't been drunk. The problem, Oscar said, was that the foreman had made his dad use a faulty ladder.

Near the end of the third day, a doctor arrived. "What's wrong with him?" José asked.

"Your father suffered a concussion, which led to bleeding in the brain and resulted in a coma," the doctor explained. José tried his best to understand the doctor's words. "The good news is that he should

come out of it. But when he does, things won't be the same. He fell on his left side, so when he wakes up, there will be damage to his right side. What I don't understand is why he wasn't treated here immediately." The doctor paged through the notes in his dad's patient file. "Looks as though the nurse thought you were saying he was intoxicated. If we would've understood you, we could've treated him sooner, and the damage would be less."

15

José sat slumped in the chair in Mrs. Baker's office. His dad was back home and José was back at school, but that was about the only good news in José's shuffled life. While Mrs. Baker understood José missing school to be with his father at the hospital, his boss at Rainbow did not. Despite his record of working hard every minute, his boss fired him over the phone for being unreliable.

"You'll have to make up your assignments," Mrs. Baker said. José nodded in agreement.

"But it isn't just school you've missed," Mrs. Baker continued. "Even before your father went into the hospital, I noticed you weren't attending after-school tutoring. Why not?"

"I'm too busy."

"José, that's no excuse," Mrs. Baker snapped. She seemed angry. "You have to learn to set priorities. Make good choices."

Another nod, but it was mostly out of habit. He had no good alternatives.

"You're doing well in language arts. What's different about that class for you?" Mrs. Baker asked. "Maybe you could think about that and then apply it to other classes."

"I think it's the book we're reading. I guess I can relate to it some way."

"I know that's harder in other classes, so here's what I want to do. I want you to attend after-school tutoring like you promised, and—"

"I don't think I can," José said. "I lost my job at Rainbow, and I need those job credits. I'm going to call up Mr. Harmon at UPS.

Maybe he can take me on again, part-time after school."

"Okay, that's fair. So here's what we'll do. Do you know Kayla Robins?"

"Some."

"Mr. Hunter says Kayla is interested in becoming a science teacher. She can start with you," Mrs. Baker said. "I'll talk with her about tutoring you during advisory. She would earn credits too."

José looked at the floor and nodded.

"You've dug yourself in deep, José, but Rondo is the ladder that's gonna help you rise up." Mrs. Baker encouraged him until the bell rang, when she added, "Work on being on time, okay? We start at eight o'clock, not eight fifteen!"

José took his seat in language arts just as Mrs. Howard-Hernandez was starting up.

"Today we'll read 'Ghost Soldiers,' and then we'll break into pairs for an assignment." The teacher read the story about O'Brien being shot. After she finished, she said, "Who can tell me the theme of this story?"

José raised his hand. Mrs. Howard-Hernandez appeared stunned by the rare sight. "José?"

"I think O'Brien realizes that the pain of a gunshot isn't actually as bad as the fear of being shot."

"That's exactly right," Mrs. Howard-Hernandez said with a smile. "Building up a fear of something is often worse than actually experiencing it."

José couldn't smile back. All he could think of was the secret he'd been keeping from his family for so long. Was O'Brien right? Was the fear of pain worse than the pain itself?

16

After he picked up his father from physical therapy, José stopped at Rainbow to pick up his last paycheck. He hoped he wouldn't see his old boss. José wondered, based on his experience at Rainbow and his father's with Benson Roofing, if most bosses were jerks and cowards.

José asked his father to stay in the car. He didn't plan to be long or talk to anyone.

"What happened to you, José?" asked

Angelica Cruz, a pretty girl stocking fruit, when she saw him enter the store. He quickly told her why he got fired. "That's not right."

"I know, but he's the boss," José replied. "He gets to make the rules."

"It's still not fair," Angelica said, which was true of most of the boss's rules.

"Let me tell you what else isn't fair," José said, and he told Angelica a little bit about his life. She stopped what she was doing and listened intently. He wondered if the sensitive-guy vibe he gave off—not an act, as it was for some of his friends—was winning him points. "So, it's been a rough week, I guess you could say," he finished.

"That's terrible, José."

"I'm just here to pick up my last paycheck, so I guess I won't see you again." José let the words dangle like bait, but Angelica didn't bite or ask for his number. "I guess I'd better go."

José began to walk away, but then he heard Angelica call his name.

He turned around and tried to dazzle her with his best smile. However, she wasn't paying attention. "José, isn't that your father?" Angelica pointed at his dad, standing by a pile of mangos. His father wiped the fruit against his dirty shirt and then took a bite out of it.

"¿Qué estás haciendo?" José asked, running over to him. His father just chewed faster. *It's like being with a child*, José thought, *except a child will learn, but Dad can't. We're stuck in time.*

◦ ◦ ◦

After dinner, José stood outside the apartment when he made the call to his boss at UPS. He hoped to leave a message and avoid begging for a job like he'd seen his dad do many times.

"Hello, this is Bob Harmon." It wasn't a message.

"Mr. Harmon, this is José Gomez. How are you?" *What was he doing there now?*

"Busy, José, always busy. I was just thinking about you. What can I do for you?"

"I'd like to come back." There was no need to tell him about losing his Rainbow job.

"Well, that's very good news for me," Mr. Harmon said. "You are one of the hardest workers I've known." José smiled. *Okay, that's one boss who wasn't a jerk or coward,* he thought.

"I could even start tonight if you wanted," José offered.

Mr. Harmon paused. Didn't he want José back? "Well, the thing about it is that I'm not a foreman on third shift anymore. I got promoted," Mr. Harmon said. José thought he sounded proud. Good for him. "I'm a manager on first shift."

"Well, maybe you could put in a good word about me with—"

"I was hoping you'd call, José, because I'd like you to come back and start training to be a foreman. What do you say? Would you like that?"

It was a no-brainer. José knew foremen made a lot more money. "Very much, Mr. Harmon."

"I'll see you Monday. We start at eight a.m. sharp. You've made a good choice, José."

17

The doctor asked José more questions about his father's condition after the fall (slurred speech, sick to his stomach, and forgetting things). Then he left José alone with his crying mother and unmoving father. The second the door closed, José's mom began asking José questions about what the doctor had said, but José couldn't answer them. If only he had told the nurses, "he hurt his head, and his stomach hurts too," or anything else. But his dad kept saying "intoxicado," so that was the word Jose used.

José asked his mom to be quiet. He needed time put it together, like a math story problem at school. He'd used that word not knowing that in English, intoxicated *meant drunk. The doctor had explained how some symptoms of a concussion, like slurred speech, could be mistaken sometimes for being drunk. José realized his word choice had caused the nurses to call the police instead of admitting him to the hospital to be treated. Instead of spending the night in a hospital bed with nurses checking on him, José guessed his father had spent the night sleeping on the cold floor of a jail cell.*

José blamed himself but also the nurses, for not knowing better, and the police. They were just like his dad's foreman; they all seemed to assume his dad was drunk. José overheard how people talked: he was Mexican, after all, he must be drunk to be acting that way. José hated Benson, hated Minnesota, and hated the United States. He hated everything, but mostly himself.

His father had worked ten hours a day for the roofer. His mother worked twelve hours at two jobs. All José had to do was one simple thing: be the bridge between his parents and the English-speaking world around them. He had failed, and now his family paid the price.

"¿José, qué dijo el doctor?" *his mom asked.*

"What did the doctor say?" José repeated. Then he managed a smile and lied to his mom's crying face.

18

Angelica was right about things being unfair.
Yes, it was unfair that José got fired. But the
greater unfairness lay in how his dad struggled
to do something that came easy to everyone
else: smile.

His father didn't know it, but José had asked
the therapist to help his father learn to smile
again, or at least something like it. A person
could live with one hand or one leg, but not

without the ability to show happiness. Especially if there was limited happiness in his dad's life.

"*Este está bueno,*" José said as he handed his dad the big piece of scrap metal. From the date in his father's notebook, he'd found the fine piece of metal the day before he fell at home. His father admired the piece of scrap, his eyes going back and forth, inspecting every inch.

José took off his glove and touched the cold metal. Goose bumps crossed over José's arm from a thought that wouldn't leave his mind. All the talk in language arts about the difference between memories and stories, about separating fact from fiction, had got him thinking. Everything had a past, present, and future. This metal had once held up a house, but now it was scrap, no longer serving a purpose. Yet, in the near future, it would be melted down and used to make new metals to hold up another house and serve a purpose again. José knew his own shadowed past all too well.

José's father motioned that it was time to move on, so they began walking slowly toward the next address, the next stop in their journey. Along the way, José spoke with his father slowly, telling him the choices he faced and asking his father for his wisdom. His dad's brain might be damaged, but José hoped his father's heart stayed strong and his wisdom remained intact.

He asked his father about small things like Angelica. His dad told him not to be discouraged, and he made José laugh with a story about meeting José's mother. As they neared the final address in the book, José asked the hardest question: what should he do? He could work first shift as a foreman in training at UPS, but the job meant he'd have to drop out of Rondo. He'd make more money, so his dad could get physical therapy more than once a week, and maybe they could get a bigger place. *Or maybe I could move out*, José thought, *and be free.*

"*Haz lo correcto*," his father said. But that was the problem, José thought: both of them were the right choices. How did a person decide between two good options? On another matter, though, his father was correct—José needed to do what was right, and what was right was to tell the truth. José hoped the shadow of shame chasing him would go away if he admitted what really happened ten years ago.

○ ○ ○

"*Lo siento mucho*," José said, his voice breaking. In the other room, Cecilia's children were sleeping; around the table, José's family sat in stone silence as José explained his mistake at the hospital and the consequences. He knew Jesus forgave all sins, but would his family?

For the longest time, no one spoke. Finally, his mother rose and went into the other room. Seconds later, José heard the sound of prayers.

Cecilia pushed back her chair, rose, and stood next to José. She gently kissed him on the top of the head and told him not to worry, that everyone makes mistakes. The important thing was learning from them. She said she was trying, but she knew it wasn't easy. *Nothing in our lives is ever easy*, he thought. They'd need to stay strong, stay together, and stay focused on the hopes and dreams they carried with them.

19

"You're late," the man's voice said, sharply. José looked at the clock on the wall. 8:15.

José nervously picked at his wool cap, still wet with snow. The Chevy didn't start, the bus was late arriving, and José knew he'd now face the consequences. "I'm sorry, Mr. H."

"Have a seat."

José put a hand over his mouth to cover his yawn. This was not the impression he wanted to make on what felt like the first day of something new.

"You best not be late for me, José, or else," Kayla's voice called out. Laugher filled José's first-period science class, but José was distracted by the buzzing of his phone. Mr. Harmon was calling, probably in response to the message José had left him saying he couldn't take the first-shift job after all. José turned off the phone, took his seat at the table, and listened with his fellow Rondo students as Mr. Hunter explained the science project they would be doing in class. Unlike the hard chairs in the hospital and on the bus, the chair at Rondo felt safe and soft to José.

◦ ◦ ◦

"I'm sorry Mr. Harmon," José said when he called back. "I promised Mrs. Baker, my parents, and everybody that I'd stay in school. I'll come to work second and third, but I want to finish school. You understand?"

Even through the phone, José could hear the hustle and bustle of the UPS warehouse. Standing just outside the school door during the short morning break, José also heard the sounds of Rondo, a mix of languages and lives that all came together in one place.

"If you work those shifts, it's just moving boxes, not foreman training. Don't you want to get ahead?" Mr. Harmon asked.

José stifled a laugh. He was a nineteen-year-old eleventh-grader. *I don't want to get ahead*, he thought, *I just want to get caught up*. "Yes, but I need to finish school. That's my choice."

"You're sure."

"Positive."

"Well, I'll tell human resources. They'll call about the other shifts. Good luck, José."

◊ ◊ ◊

"Good luck, everyone," Mrs. Howard-Hernandez said as she handed out the final exam on *The Things They Carried*. Like the other tests, it was a combination of short-answer questions and one long essay. José blew through the short answers, writing quickly. He knew the material, but he also wanted to spend time on the essay question. The second she'd told the class to turn the test over, José's eyes went to the bottom line. He was ready to answer.

The question read, "One of our first assignments was listing things that people carry. Real things they carry in a bag, things they carry because of their culture, and the emotional things they carry. Has reading this book changed the things you carry? What will you carry forward from this book?"

José clutched the pencil for a second like it was a piece of scrap metal with a past, a present, and a future. His mind flashed on his dad, before the accident and after. He wrote:

What I will carry from this story is hope. Tim is in a terrible situation in this book, caught up in a war he didn't want to fight in a place he didn't want to be. But he had no choice, because he had responsibilities. Sometimes responsibilities burden you, but mostly they make you stronger. You show the world—and yourself— you can handle the things you carry.

For years I carried a fear with me, a fear of letting out a secret, a mistake I'd made. I knew I could never be free of that weight until I told the secret. And O'Brien was right, the fear was far worse than the outcome. I had expected shame, but instead I received forgiveness. And in forgiveness is hope for a better future.

All of the characters in the book carry heavy physical loads, but they also carry weighty emotional loads, including grief, fear, and love. After the war, the psychological burdens the men carried during the war continued to define them. Those who survive carry guilt, grief, and confusion, and many of the stories in the collection are about these survivors' attempts to come to terms with their experience. And maybe it is O'Brien who survives the best, because he tells the story. When we tell survival stories, then we give hope to all of those suffering and in despair.

20

With his family and his new girlfriend, Angelica, beside him, José applauded as Rondo students walked across the makeshift stage to get their diplomas. Some students he'd known for years, while others had come to Rondo only for one semester.

"I'm so happy for them," José whispered to Angelica. She squeezed his hand; he squeezed back. On his other side, he did the same. He squeezed his father's right hand, and even if he could barely discern it, José thought his father had squeezed back. The third-shift UPS wages had bought more therapy but provided José with less sleep. While he came to school tired, he pushed through it, and as he watched his fellow classmates accept hard-earned diplomas, he knew why.

"You've dug yourself in deep," José remembered Mrs. Baker telling him, "But Rondo is the ladder that's gonna help you rise up." Not only was the ladder of Rondo strong, it was also well supported. Mrs. Baker, Mr. Hunter, Mrs. Howard-Hernandez, all of the staff and aides held firm to the bottom of the ladder so that students could climb.

"They look proud," Aunt Cecilia said in accented English. In his rare spare time, José had agreed to watch Cecilia's children more, but only if she took English classes. José knew a family like his needed more than one bridge.

José looked at the teachers onstage. Mrs. Howard-Hernandez was second from the end. José made a mental note to tell her that, come this day next year, he'd have two more items to add to the list of things he carried: a high school diploma and a college acceptance letter.

SPANISH TO ENGLISH

GLOSSARY

ambulancia: ambulance

¡A ver si puedes cerrar las piernas esta vez!: Let's see if you can keep your legs closed this time!

¡basta, ya párenle!: enough, stop it already!

Este está bueno: This is a good one

Haz lo correcto: Do what is right

intoxicado: sick due to food poisoning

Lo siento mucho: I'm sorry

Mamá, ¿qué pasó?: Mom, what happened?

Papi, ¿estás bien?: Daddy, are you okay?

pinche: lousy (slang)

Porque somos familia, hijo: Because we're family, son

¿Qué dijo el doctor?: What did the doctor say?

¿Qué estás haciendo?: What are you doing?

¿Quién te va a cuidar a los niños?: Who's going to watch the kids for you?

rápido, rápido: fast, quickly

Te necesito: I need you

Todo va a estar bien: Everything will be fine

Tu papá tuvo un accidente: Your dad had an accident

vaquero: cowboy

Ven aquí por favor: Please come here

AUTHOR'S NOTE

I began writing this book after a conversation with my friend Marcela. I knew I wanted to write about a young man who acted as the "bridge" between the English-speaking world and the Spanish-only world of his parents. As we discussed this, Marcela talked about how often translations by children are flawed. Not only did they often take place in times of great stress, such as a medical emergency, but the children were also translating words and concepts that were too adult for them to understand.

Marcela also helped me develop the characters, the setting, and a good part of the plot. In addition, she reviewed the Spanish. It is always tricky to write about or from the point of view of a different culture. In this book, I tried to be sensitive in portraying this culture.

In addition to my own research on concussions, Brent Chartier—who has coauthored books with me—brought his expertise from working with the one of the leading neurosurgeons in the United States. The medical mistranslation portrayed in this book is based on the famous 1980 Willie Ramirez case. As a result of an interpreting error at a Florida hospital, Willie's brain hemorrhage was misdiagnosed, and he was left quadriplegic.

The lesson plan for *The Things They Carried* quoted in the text was created by Lisa Seppelt.

Finally, as with all the books in The Alternative series, students and teachers at South St. Paul Community Learning Center read and commented on the manuscript, in particular John Egelkrout, Mindy Haukedahl, Kathleen Johnson, and Lisa Seppelt.

ABOUT THE AUTHOR

Patrick Jones is the author of more than twenty novels for teens. He has also written two nonfiction books about combat sports: *The Main Event*, on professional wrestling, and *Ultimate Fighting*, on mixed martial arts. He has spoken to students at more than one hundred alternative schools, including residents of juvenile correctional facilities. Find him on the web at www.connectingya.com and on Twitter: @PatrickJonesYA.

THE ALTERNATIVE

FAILING CLASSES.

DROPPING OUT.

JAIL TIME.

When it seems like there are no other options left,
Rondo Alternative High School might just be the
last chance a student needs.

THE ALTERNATIVE

BARRIER
PATRICK JONES

THE ALTERNATIVE

BRIDGE
PATRICK JONES

THE ALTERNATIVE

CONTROLLED.
PATRICK JONES

THE ALTERNATIVE

OUTBURST
PATRICK JONES

THE ALTERNATIVE

TARGET
PATRICK JONES

IT'S THE OPPORTUNITY OF A LIFETIME—
IF YOU CAN HANDLE IT.

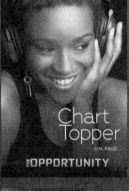

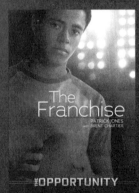

THE OPPORTUNITY

WELCOME TO

THE DOJO

BODY SHOT
PATRICK JONES

SIDE CONTROL
PATRICK JONES

LEARN TO FIGHT,
LEARN TO LIVE,
AND LEARN
TO FIGHT
FOR YOUR
LIFE.

HEAD KICK
PATRICK JONES

TRIANGLE CHOKE
PATRICK JONES